EGMONT

We bring stories to life

First published in Great Britain 2011 by Egmont UK Limited
239 Kensington High Street, London W8 6SA

Text copyright © Portobello Rights Limited 2011
Illustrations © Portobello Rights Limited and the BBC 2011,
taken from the BBC series 'World of Happy by Giles Andreae'
based on original illustrations by Janet Cronin

Giles Andreae has asserted his moral rights

A CIP catalogue record for this title is available from the British Library

ISBN 978 1 4052 5841 8
1 3 5 7 9 10 8 6 4 2
Printed in Italy

a story about CELEBRATING our DIFFERENCES

my name is ....

and special things that make me different are

....

....

The World of Dogs was run with great EFFICIENCY.

There were
MACHINES for
every kind of task.

And the most brilliant was the one
that dealt with all the BUSINESS
that a dog might leave behind.

But there are many different KINDS of dog and one machine could not ACCOMMODATE them all.

"The dogs must CHANGE," decreed the King. "The business of each dog henceforth must fit PRECISELY into this excellent machine."

But some dogs simply could not manage . . .

and the King became most FURIOUS indeed.

Until one little dog declared, "This is not right, O King. We dogs should not be SHAPED by your machine."

"We come in DIFFERENT sizes, different forms.

That is the WONDER of us dogs.
That is what DOGNESS is."

And all the other dogs rose up and cried . . .

"Let us overthrow this dog and make YOU King!"

And now each dog can shape his OWN machine.

For every dog IS different. And that is WHY their world is such a HAPPY place to be.